Class Action

by Brad Slaight

D1197122

Baker's Plays
7611 Sunset Blvd.
Los Angeles, CA 90042
bakersplays.com

Class Action was written for and first produced by the Young Conservatory at the American Conservatory Theater (Carey Perloff, Artistic Director; Craig Slaight, Young Conservatory Director) San Francisco, California, in May of 1994. The play was Directed by Amy Mueller; Assistant Director/Piano Accompaniment by Nick Edwards; Lighting Design by Kelly Roberson.

The ensemble cast was as follows:

Kierstin Barile
Danton Char
Samer Danfoura
Natalie Lee
Sarah Palmer
Maria Sideris
Richard Tayloe

The playwright wishes to thank Craig Slaight and Amy Mueller for their invaluable guidance and suggestions.

PLAYWRIGHT'S NOTE:

The many scenes in *Class Action* collectively make up the "play". Although each scene stands on its own, there is a common thread here -- All of the scenes deal with situations that take place outside the classroom. It is my opinion that these events are sometimes the most important experiences young people deal with in High School.

Staging this play can be done as simply or as complex as you wish to make it. I have purposely avoided using a gimmick to connect the many scenes and strongly suggest that you stage the transitions from scene to scene, without using standard blackouts, to keep the play moving along. The scenes are arranged in a "suggested order", however you may find it necessary to change the order and/or omit some of them.

-- Brad Slaight

SUGGESTED CAST:
7 STUDENTS - 4 WOMEN, 3 MEN

OPTIONAL CAST:
Depending on your casting needs, and since there are many scenes and characters, you may choose to use more or less than the suggested cast.

THE SET:
An open playing area containing several boxes and benches, which can be used as suggestive set pieces. Other elements may be added, depending on your tastes and resources. (In the original production the Director placed several standing school lockers upstage, incorporating them into some of the scenes.)

MUSIC:
You may want to add transitional music between scenes, as well as sound effects and mood music during the scenes.

COSTUMES:
Basic school clothes and suggestive props (glasses, hats, etc.)

TIME:
The present.

PLACE:
A modern High School.

CLASS ACTION

(OPENING: the CAST is on-stage as the audience enters. It should appear that they are in class and reading out of textbooks, or writing. When it's time to start the show, a BELL is heard. The CAST will begin to disperse and talk among themselves, as if class has been dismissed. The HOUSE LIGHTS fade, as the stage LIGHTS come up.)

SCENE 1

(BETH and LISA enter from opposite sides and meet in the middle of the stage.)

BETH. Lisa!
LISA. Beth!
BETH. News?
LISA. Nothing.
BETH. Carl?
LISA. No!
BETH. David?
LISA. David!
BETH. Date?
LISA. Called.
BETH. Really?
LISA. Really.
BETH. And?
LISA. Possible.
BETH. Lucky.

LISA. Hopeful.

BETH. Parents?

LISA. Clue-less.

BETH. Risky.

LISA. Right.

BETH. When?

LISA. Saturday.

BETH. Where?

LISA. Mall.

BETH. Sneaky.

LISA. Genius.

BETH. Happy?

LISA. You?

BETH. Brad.

LISA. Double?

BETH. Maybe.

LISA. Party.

BETH. Brad?

LISA. Right.

BETH. Embarrassing.

LISA. Sorry.

BETH. Tommy.

LISA. Tommy?

BETH. Hoping.

LISA. Good. *(A BELL is heard.)*

LISA. Damn.

BETH. Already.

LISA. Algebra.

BETH. Choir.

LISA. Lucky.

BETH. 'Bye.

LISA. Later. *(They both exit.)*

SCENE 2

(KAREN and LEON sit in desks, back to back; nothing is said for a few moments.)

LEON. What time is it now?

KAREN. Two minutes later than the last time you asked me.

LEON. Oh, yeah. *(Long pause.)* I've never been in detention before.

KAREN. You already told me that.

LEON. Oh, yeah.

KAREN. But you didn't tell me why you're here.

LEON. Is it important?

KAREN. You're doin' time -- let's hear the crime.

LEON. I pulled the fire alarm Tuesday.

KAREN. *(Impressed.)* That was you?

LEON. That was me.

KAREN. A guy like you – I'll bet you thought there really was a fire.

LEON. No, I knew there wasn't.

KAREN. Well, well – Little Leon Mosher has a bad side to him. Why did you do it? Mad at a teacher? Stressed out by the system?

LEON. Well, uh -- none of the above.

KAREN. This ain't a multiple-choice test, Mosher. If it wasn't one of those reasons, why'd you do it?

LEON. You'll just laugh at me.

KAREN. Probably, but give it a shot.

LEON. I did it so I could get a chance to be with you. *(KAREN stares at him for a moment.)* You're not laughing.

KAREN. You're right.

LEON. You see, I've always wanted to talk to you, away from the crowd you hang with – Ever since we were kids, but you're never alone.

KAREN. So I have a lot of friends, you got a problem with that?

LEON. I know you're different when you're away from the others. You pretend to be so tough and everything, but I know you're not like that.

KAREN. Is that right?

LEON. I may seem like a real dork to you, but one thing I pride myself on is that I know people. I can see through the fake sincerity of Sue Powell our Homecoming Queen, and I can also see the beautiful person beneath your tough talk and ever present scowl. And I mean that as a compliment. *(She turns around and stares at him for a moment.)*

KAREN. Let me get this straight – You got yourself two weeks of detention just to be with me?

LEON. Yes. *(Long pause.)* I wanted to ask you out on a date. Nothing major, just a coke or something. Like, maybe after detention today?

KAREN. A date? Just you and me?

LEON. That's what I was hoping for. *(KAREN thinks for a moment.)*

KAREN. All right, Leon, but just one coke. Only because you pulled the alarm, and I like stuff like that.

LEON. Without all your friends?

KAREN. Like I'd want them to know.

LEON. You got a point there. *(Long pause.)* What time is it now?

KAREN. Don't push your luck, Leon.

LEON. Oh, yeah.

SCENE 3

(ANDREA paces, while NINA sits writing on a yellow note-pad with a pencil.)

ANDREA. What do we have so far?

NINA. Just the title.

ANDREA. We've been working on this stupid story for over two hours and all we have is a title?

NINA. And even that sucks.

ANDREA. I kinda like it.

NINA. "The Perfect Guy?"

ANDREA. It's got a certain mystery about it.

NINA. Yeah, the mystery is we're never gonna finish this story. It's due tomorrow.

ANDREA. All right, let's quit arguing and start writing.

NINA. How about this? *(She writes.)* "It was a dark stormy night when I heard the knock at my door." *(We hear a knock.)* "A stranger walked in -- he had a hunchback and limped badly." *(One of the MALE PLAYERS limps in, wearing a hump.)*

ANDREA. No way. Not a hunchback. Make him more romantic.

NINA. *(She erases part of what she has written, the HUNCHBACK exits.)* "A stranger walked in, he was a young handsome man -- "

ANDREA. With a thick English accent! *(Another MALE PLAYER enters.)*

YOUNG MAN. *(Thick English accent.)* Pardon me, mates -- I've had a bit of an accident with my jalopy and need to call a bobby.

NINA. I hate foreign accents. *(Writes.)* "He was a well

spoken guy from the mid-west."

YOUNG MAN. Excuse me, ladies, my Camaro threw a rod and I gotta call Triple A.

ANDREA. I want an English guy.

NINA. You should have thought about that before you made me do all the writing.

ANDREA. All right, so he needs to use the phone. Uh -- oh, I know. The phone is out because of the storm.

NINA. Good. "Suddenly the power goes out." *(LIGHTS flicker; then fade, but not all the way.)*

ANDREA. Just because the power goes out, doesn't mean the phone is dead.

NINA. Oh yeah, watch this. "He crosses to the phone and picks it up, but -- "

YOUNG MAN. Phone's dead. Must be because of the storm.

ANDREA. I don't know --

NINA. Trust me, Andrea, it works.

ANDREA. So then he decides that he has to stay the night with us.

NINA. *(Writes.)* "He turns and faces the two girls."

YOUNG MAN. Look, do you think I could stay here for the night?

ANDREA. This is getting interesting -- How about, "The two girls light some candles and get to know him better."

NINA. I got a better idea. *(Writes.)* "Realizing he will be staying the night, he looks at the two girls more closely. He crosses to Andrea -- " *(The YOUNG MAN crosses to ANDREA, she flirts with him with her eyes.)*

NINA. "A nice girl, but rather plain, he thinks to himself."

ANDREA. Hey!

NINA. "He then casts his eyes on Nina, drinking her

vision, dazzled by her beauty. Crosses to her and reaches for her hand." *(The YOUNG MAN crosses to NINA, takes her hand and kisses it gently.)*

YOUNG MAN. "You are totally beautiful."

ANDREA. Nina, this is supposed to be our story. And besides he's a Perfect Guy, not *your* perfect guy. *(NINA continues to write frantically.)*

NINA. "He is so overcome with Nina that he sweeps her up in his arms – *(HE picks her up.)* "And carries her out of the room, down the hall, where they kiss passionately for the rest of the stormy evening!" *(THEY start to exit, NINA tears the pages off the note-pad and discards the unused portion to the floor as they leave.)*

ANDREA. Nina, wait – what about the assignment? Nina! *(ANDREA picks up the note-pad.)*

ANDREA. All right, I'll just write the story myself and you can flunk. *(She pauses to think, then starts to write.)*

ANDREA. "It was late fall when Andrea's boyfriend from *England* came to visit." *(We hear a knock on the door; she opens it and another actor enters. Writing.)* "She was a little mad at him for being late, but when he showed her the roses, she smiled and forgave him." *(HE holds up a dozen roses, previously hidden behind his back.)*

ENGLISH YOUNG MAN. *(With accent.)* "Lovely to see you, my little bird."

ANDREA. "This was going to be a night that they would both remember for a long, long time – "

SCENE 4

(DANIELLE enters. She places her hand on her womb area.)

DANIELLE. I haven't started to show yet, so most everyone thinks that I'm moody because I broke up with Richie. That's partly true, although I don't blame him for not wanting the burden of having this kid. We're both only 17. He wanted me to "take care of it", and even though I believe in the whole choice thing, my choice was to keep her. Oh, I know it will be a "girl" because I'm hardly sick or anything, and my Aunt Susan told me that it's always baby boys that make a pregnant woman nauseous. She should know -- she had four. My Aunt Susan's been real cool about this. I told her before I told anybody, because we've always had a special friendship. Richie doesn't talk to me much anymore, and I'm sure some of my friends are going to be pretty weird around me when I start swelling. But somehow none of that seems to matter. I know that I'll be able to handle all the problems that come along because there is someone who is much more important than all of them put together. And she is inside me now. Waiting to help me. Waiting to need me.

SCENE 5

(JACK, a jock type, sits and writes in a notebook; hides it when he sees JONI.)

JONI. I saw you writing in your notebook, you can't fool me.

JACK. Hi, Joni.

JONI. You haven't finished your English assignment, have you?

JACK. Not really.

JONI. I know you so well, Jack Heller.

JACK. Yeah —

JONI. You always wait until the last minute.

JACK. What were we 'spose to do?

JONI. Poetry! Remember, we have to turn in a poem? Mrs. Vernon only told us five or six times.

JACK. Guess my head was somewhere else.

JONI. Want to hear mine?

JACK. Sure. *(JONI takes a paper out and reads from it proudly.)*

JONI. "LOVE by Joni Mendez"
I was riding in my car,
I was riding all alone
I was riding in my car
Going through the radar zone.
The policeman clocked my speed,
At 80 miles per hour
He asked me why I sped like that
Calling me a wild flower.
So I told him that I hadn't seen
My guy for over a week
And I was rushing to see him
So the two of us could speak.
The cop he smiled and said okay
He understood my longing heart.
And let me continue on my way.
So my love and me would no longer be apart.

JACK. Wow — that's great.

JONI. I guess I just have a way with words.

JACK. Wish I could write like that.

JONI. You just concentrate on winning the game tonight. I've already taken care of your assignment -- I wrote your poem for you. So you can stop worrying.

JACK. Really? *(She holds up paper.)*

JONI. It's called "Broken Heart" and it's almost as good as the one I wrote for myself. I better hold it for you until class, you'll probably lose it. *(SHE kisses him on the cheek, and then exits. JACK makes sure she is gone; opens his note-book up and reads from it.)*

JACK. "Winterscape. A Poem by Jack Heller."

A vibrant glaze slips upon the busy hillside
blowing a blue chill like notes from
an angry saxophone
upon the unsuspecting hollow heart world
hunkering down the brown leaf child of fall
and causing a pond frog to scream
his protest at the dormant mud.
And with a simple dark shade
Closes the lid
Closes the winterscape
Closes the world
For now.

(JACK tears the poem from his notebook; shoves it in his back pocket. Picks up his notebook and spins his football in the air as he exits.)

SCENE 6

(TINA and ROBBY sit close together, as if they are parked in a car. Their position is romantic, but their expressions are not.)

TINA. Haven't we been here long enough?

ROBBY. I say we give it another five minutes. *(Pause.)* Look who just pulled up –

TINA. That surprises you? Gale and Lyle come up here to make out all the time.

ROBBY. I know – I just thought that tonight maybe they'd get a motel room or somethin'. *(Pause.)*

TINA. This dress has some kind of wires in the bra – it's starting to cut into my skin.

ROBBY. Yeah, well this tuxedo sucks. I told the guy the cumberbum was too small.

TINA. Cummerbund -- it's called a cummerbund.

ROBBY. Whatever – it's too small.

TINA. Just take it off.

ROBBY. Hey, with what I paid for it I'm gonna wear it until I take it back. *(TINA nudges him and nods toward another part of the stage.)*

TINA. Look, Susie and Tom are doin' it.

ROBBY. How can you tell?

TINA. The fact that their car is rocking back and forth is a pretty good clue.

ROBBY. Think we should get this thing rockin', too? *(She gives him a look.)*

ROBBY. I didn't mean for real, I meant pretend – like we've been doin' all night.

TINA. Nah, people would really get suspicious then.

We've never even dated before.

ROBBY. I don't see why we have to pretend at all. Why don't we just tell everyone that we didn't want to go to the prom alone, so we decided to go together?

TINA. Because that makes us both look like a couple of losers.

ROBBY. We are a couple of losers.

TINA. Speak for yourself. *(Pause; suddenly ROBBY pulls her in tight.)*

TINA. What are you doing?

ROBBY. Karla and Jonathan are just two cars away -- they can see us.

TINA. So?

ROBBY. So, I asked Karla to go to the prom with me and she turned me down. I don't want her to think we're just sittin' up here.

TINA. She turned you down? Who does she think she is?

ROBBY. Yeah, right. Who does she think she is? *(Pause.)* Man, I feel so stupid.

TINA. How do you think I feel?

ROBBY. Hey, you could have at least gone with another girl. Lots of 'em paired off. But if I went with a buddy, I'd be gay. Talk about your double standards. *(She nudges him again.)*

TINA. Look, Connie and Tim are making out and this is only their second date.

ROBBY. Yeah, two weeks ago they didn't even know each other. *(ROBBY looks at TINA for a moment.)*

TINA. By the way, the corsage is very nice. I'll reimburse you for it tomorrow.

ROBBY. No hurry.

TINA. Minus what I paid for your boutonniere.

ROBBY. My what?

TINA. The flower I gave you.

ROBBY. Oh, right. *(Pause.)*

ROBBY. Uh – maybe we should, you know – you know.

TINA. No I don't know. Maybe we should what?

ROBBY. Well, if anyone is lookin' at us, like we're lookin' at them – I thought maybe we should kiss or something.

TINA. I don't know?

ROBBY. Only a pretend kiss.

TINA. You may be right – it would certainly remove any doubt, in case we are being watched.

ROBBY. All right, go ahead.

TINA. You're the guy, you're suppose to be the kisser – I'm the kissee.

ROBBY. Right. *(ROBBY awkwardly puts his arm around her; gives her a quick peck on the lips.)*

TINA. I get more romantic kisses from my little brother. If you're gonna do it – do it right. *(ROBBY hesitates, then really lays one on her; a long, compassionate kiss. When they come up for air, they've both been affected by it. Overwhelmed.)* That was better.

ROBBY. *(Also affected.)* Yeah. *(Pause.)*

TINA. Look, there's Melanie. Maybe we should kiss again so – *(Before she can finish her sentence, ROBBY kisses her again. Even longer than before. Finally they pull away from each other and recover.)*

ROBBY. *(Looking at watch.)* Well, I think it would be okay if we left now.

TINA. We've certainly proved our point.

ROBBY. Yes we have. *(ROBBY reaches to start the car.)*

TINA. You start that car and you're a dead man! *(TINA pulls him in for another kiss.)*

SCENE 7

(NATE enters, bouncing a basketball.)

NATE. He shoots, he scores! *(He makes a sound of fans cheering.)* The excitement of the game is everything to me. I think it goes back to when I was three and my Uncle Joey gave me a Fisher-Price toy hoop and ball. My Mom says I wouldn't play with any of my other toys after that. It was throw the ball in the hoop, pick up the ball, throw the ball in the hoop, pick up the ball -- all day long. When I was ten, my Dad put a backboard and hoop up over the garage. I made him make it regulation, even though it was way too high for me. I only made maybe one in ten shots. But I practiced every day, and dreamed about basketball every night. I sat on the bench most of Junior High, hoping that I would soon grow and I could be a first stringer. But I didn't grow. My Doctor says I'm a late bloomer, it may not even happen until I'm eighteen or nineteen. Great. So, since our school doesn't have a horse racing team in need of a jockey, and since I'm still addicted to basketball, I signed on as the team's Manager. Hey, it's not so bad. I still get the best seat at all the games. I still get to be in the team picture and I still get to be around basketball. The excitement of the game is everything to me.

SCENE 8

(LAURA sits at a library study table. MELANIE and JANINE enter and sit next to her. Other STUDENTS people the scene and will "shush" occasionally when the conversations get too loud. MIKE enters and notices

*LAURA with her friends; decides to sit with SCOOTER
at a nearby table.)*

MELANIE. I can't believe the cafeteria served mystery meat
three days in a row. Wonder what we ate today?

LAURA. I think it was pork.

JANINE. It might have just been bad chicken.

MELANIE. Eee-yo. *(MELANIE looks at JANINE.)*

JANINE. You know, I heard the weirdest rumor about you,
Laura.

MELANIE. I heard it, too.

LAURA. Really?

JANINE. Somebody said they saw you out on a date last
night with that fat kid Mike Howard. *(JANINE notices MIKE.)*
Oh God, he's sitting right over there. *(LAURA reacts.)*

MELANIE. We told them that you were both in the school
play and were probably just practicing your lines.

JANINE. That had to be it, right? *(They both wait for
LAURA to respond.)*

LAURA. We are both in the school play.

MELANIE. *(Relieved.)* See, I knew there was a good
reason.

LAURA. And we also went out on a date. *(Cross-cut to
MIKE and SCOOTER, who whisper at a nearby table.)*

SCOOTER. I tell you you're the King of the Misfits.
You've given every nerd in this school a reason to live.

MIKE. Is that supposed to be a compliment?

SCOOTER. Laura Rivers -- you captured the crown jewels,
baby.

STUDENT. Ssshhhh!

MIKE. You make it sound like a sport.

SCOOTER. Don't kid yourself, dating is a sport. And you

just won the Superbowl.

MIKE. I don't appreciate you making Laura sound like some kind of trophy.

SCOOTER. That's good. Sticking up for your woman is what you should be doin'.

MIKE. She's not my woman.

SCOOTER. You went out with her, didn't you?

MIKE. We went to a movie together. That's all.

SCOOTER. That's all? You make it sound like she'd go to a movie with just anybody. *(Back to LAURA, MELANIE, and JANINE.)*

JANINE. The two of you have nothing in common. You're a Senior, he's a Junior; you're popular, he's in the loser patrol; you're gorgeous, he's fat.

MELANIE. People are talking. They're calling you two "Beauty and the Beef".

LAURA. And of course you defended me because I'm your friend?

JANINE. Yes, we told them that you just feel sorry for him.

MELANIE. Because that is why you went out with him, isn't it?

LAURA. I went out with Mike Howard because he's talented, sincere and has a great sense of humor.

JANINE. You could have your pick of any guy in school.

LAURA. He's really sweet. You don't know him –

MELANIE. We don't want to know him.

JANINE. Right.

LAURA. He's very special to me.

JANINE. Special enough to ruin your whole life? Because that's what's going to happen if you keep on dating him.

LAURA. Ruin my life?

MELANIE. He's just using you, Laura. To make himself

look good. *(Back to MIKE and SCOOTER.)*

MIKE. Laura is very sweet.

SCOOTER. She's been on the cover of a magazine -- she's a model. Models aren't sweet -- they're sexy, they're dangerous, they're nasty.

MIKE. It's not like that with us.

SCOOTER. Ah-hah, you used the "us" word. This is serious.

MIKE. We're just friends.

SCOOTER. No, you and I are friends. You and Laura are lovers.

MIKE. Yeah, right.

SCOOTER. The whole school is talkin' about it.

MIKE. Yeah, I heard -- "Beauty and the Beef". *(Back to LAURA, MELANIE, and JANINE.)*

LAURA. It's bad enough that I have to get my parents' approval when I date, I shouldn't have to get my friends'.

JANINE. It's because we're friends that we're telling you this.

MELANIE. We don't want to see you get hurt.

LAURA. Jeff hurt me, Rick hurt me -- Mike Howard is the first guy I've ever gone out with that actually cares about how *I* feel.

MELANIE. If he really cares about you, he'll realize that he's wrong for you.

JANINE. Dating a guy like that can give you a bad reputation. People judge you by who you're with.

LAURA. Like when I hang out with you two?

JANINE. You know what I mean.

LAURA. So I go out on a date with someone and if others don't approve then I run the risk of losing my social position here at school?

MELANIE. You say it like you don't think it matters, but you know it does.

JANINE. This is the most important time of your life, don't screw it up.

MELANIE. We're only trying to help you. *(Back to SCOOTER and MIKE.)*

SCOOTER. They wouldn't talk if somethin' wasn't going on. And somethin' is going on – isn't it?

MIKE. Why are you pressuring me about this?

SCOOTER. Why are you avoiding the obvious?

MIKE. I don't want to push it, okay. She's the first girl who ever paid any attention to me – and I like that.

SCOOTER. I think you can get more than attention from her.

MIKE. Right now I enjoy just being with her. If I push things, I may ruin it. I may not have her love, but I have *her*. And I don't want to risk losing that.

SCOOTER. That's poetic, but it just don't work that way. *(Back to LAURA, MELANIE, and JANINE.)*

JANINE. Look, there's a party over at Kelly's house this weekend. I know for a fact that Martin Dole has been asking about you ever since you broke up with Rick. This would be the perfect time for the two of you to talk –

MELANIE. It's going to be the party of the year. Everybody will be there, it'll be the perfect time to let people know that you're, you know – *(They both look at LAURA, waiting for an answer.)*

LAURA. All right, I'll go to the party. *(They are relieved.)*

MELANIE. You've made the right decision.

JANINE. You really had us worried.

LAURA. What time should Mike and I be there? *(LAURA gets up and heads over to MIKE. Back to MIKE and*

SCOOTER.)

SCOOTER. If you don't make a play for Laura soon, she's going shopping -- and I don't mean for clothes. *(MIKE gets up and starts to leave.)* It's time to stop being logical and start being horny! *(Everyone in the library hears that. LAURA reaches an embarrassed MIKE and they exit together.)*

SCENE 9

DENNIS. *(Enters.)* My name is Dennis Gandleman. Around this school I am the object of ridicule from most of the students, simply because I have an extremely high I.Q. It's 176. My Father wanted me to enroll in a special school that deals with geniuses like myself, but Mother was firmly against that. She wanted me to have a normal education, and not be treated as some kind of freak -- Which is ironic, because that's exactly what is happening to me here. The whole concept of education is a paradox. High School is supposed to celebrate education and knowledge, but what it really celebrates is social groups and popularity. In a perfect world, a kid like me would be worshipped because of my scholastic abilities, instead of someone who can throw a 40 yard touchdown pass. I suppose I could complain, and bemoan the unfairness of it all. But I am bright. I know something that the others don't -- That, once we leave High School and enter the real world, all the rules change. What matters is power. Financial power. Power that comes from making a fortune on cutting edge computer software. Software that I am already developing. *(Pause.)* Some call me a nerd. I call myself -- ahead of my time. See you on the outside.

SCENE 10

(JONATHAN enters and spots KARLA; at the same time two other PLAYERS, BOY and GIRL enter. They stand on boxes behind JONATHAN and KARLA acting as their "subtext.")

JONATHAN. Hi Karla.

BOY. I hope she didn't find out about last night.

KARLA. *(Cold.)* Jonathan.

GIRL. You jerk.

JONATHAN. So, we still on for tonight?

BOY. I bet that big mouth Angela told her.

KARLA. That depends if you can work me into your schedule.

GIRL. How could you do this to me?

JONATHAN. You sound upset, what's goin' on?

BOY. Maybe if I just play dumb she'll drop it.

KARLA. Don't play dumb with me.

GIRL. Although for you it's very easy.

JONATHAN. Is this about me going to the Mall with Lisa?

BOY. Or was it Julie and the movies?

KARLA. You know darn well that's what I'm talking about.

GIRL. Let's see you get out of this one.

JONATHAN. I was looking for a birthday gift for you, she was helping me pick out something nice.

BOY. She's not buying it.

KARLA. Yeah, right.

GIRL. I'm not buying it.

JONATHAN. Why do you always have to be so jealous?

BOY. Why can't you just let me use you?

GIRL. That's the problem with you, you use everyone you

date.

BOY. Yeah, well at least I pay for all the dates.

GIRL. You think money is everything.

BOY. Don't start with -- *(BOY and GIRL stop arguing when they realize KARLA and JONATHAN are staring at them; the scene continues.)*

KARLA. Why do you always have to lie to me?

GIRL. I'll make him feel guilty.

JONATHAN. We're dating, it's not like we're married or anything.

BOY. She's lucky to have me at all.

KARLA. Are you saying you want to break up?

GIRL. He thinks I'm kidding.

JONATHAN. Maybe we should.

BOY. I'm calling her bluff. Any minute now she'll start crying and apologizing and I'll pretend to be hurt that she doubted me.

KARLA. Fine, here's your ring back. It never fit right anyway.

GIRL. I should have done this months ago. *(She takes the ring off and throws it at him.)*

JONATHAN. Wait a minute?

BOY. May day! May day! I'm going down. 911! 911!

KARLA. It's for the best, now we can both see whoever we want.

GIRL. Like Alan Meyers! *(KARLA exits, and the GIRL subtext leaves with her.)*

JONATHAN. Fine, it's better this way.

BOY. Don't just stand there, you idiot, go after her.

JONATHAN. Karla, wait – can't we talk about this? *(JONATHAN and BOY exit after her.)*

BOY. I can't believe she dumped me.

SCENE 11

(ARNOLD enters and stands on a chair, as if he is hiding. BILL enters and looks around.)

BILL. I know you're here in the restroom, Arnold. So don't even try to hide from me. *(ARNOLD stays frozen. BILL moves down the line, looking under each imaginary bathroom stall.)* This is like a freakin' game show. Are you behind door #1? Door #2 – *(He suddenly skips doors #3 and goes right to where ARNOLD is.)* – or door #4? *(Opens imaginary door.)* Out – NOW! *(ARNOLD steps down; BILL grabs him by the shoulders and shoves him up against a wall.)*

ARNOLD. Bill, wait – don't do it. I can explain. Just let me explain.

BILL. Make it quick, 'cause I'm kinda in a hurry and squashin' you is already cuttin' in to my fun time.

ARNOLD. I know you think I told Mrs. Pritchard that you cut out of class early when she wasn't looking, but I didn't say anything.

BILL. Then why did I hear it was you?

ARNOLD. I don't know. The only thing I can figure is that there's lots of kids in that class that don't like me. Especially after the last test when I threw off the curve by getting a perfect score while everyone else hit in the low 70's, but should I be penalized because I happen to study –

BILL. *(Cutting him off.)* Shut up. *(Pause.)* Man, no wonder everyone hates you.

ARNOLD. So you understand? Because that's how it happened. I was framed. I may be obnoxious, but I'm no tattle tale.

BILL. Tattle-tale?

ARNOLD. It's a slang word for someone who squeals on someone else.

BILL. I know what it means, I just didn't think anyone over five still used the word.

ARNOLD. It wasn't me, I swear. You're about to squash an innocent man.

BILL. Even if I believed that, it makes no difference. Word's out that it was you, so if I don't waste you then it could hurt my rep. *(BILL draws his arm back.)*

ARNOLD. Oh, I get it. Big fish eats smaller fish.

BILL. Somethin' like that.

ARNOLD. Yeah, right. And beating somebody up is the way to settle the matter. I mean that's what your Father does to you, so naturally you have to do the same to me.

BILL. What are you talkin' about?

ARNOLD. Didn't think anybody knew, did you? Well I do. I know all about what goes on over at your house. *(BILL loosens his grip.)* I spend a lot of time up on my roof at night looking through my telescope at the stars. Sometimes I get bored with the big dipper and aim my sights across the field to your house. Actually I feel sorry for you, and your Mother. The guy should be locked up, the way he treats you two. *(BILL lets go of ARNOLD. ARNOLD nervously awaits BILL's reaction.)*

ARNOLD. I shouldn't have said that. But you had me cornered. I'm sorry. It's really none of my business. *(Pause; BILL takes a few steps away.)*

BILL. He isn't always like that. But when he drinks he kinda loses it *(Pause.)* -- I don't let him go too far, and I never let him hurt Mom.

ARNOLD. Of course you don't.

BILL. My Dad hasn't worked for two years -- two years!

He keeps hopin' they'll call him back, but I think he knows they never will.

ARNOLD. Look, just punch me out and get it over with? Forget I ever mentioned it.

BILL. But you did. *(ARNOLD steps toward him, but keeps a safe distance.)*

ARNOLD. This may come as a surprise to you, but things aren't so great at my place either. The reason I spend so much time on the roof isn't because I'm that much into astronomy, it's that I'm that much into staying away from my stepmother, or as I like to call her, my "step-monster". My Dad has to work two jobs so she can sit home all day and become a preferred customer on the Home Shopping Network.

BILL. Maybe you're right -- maybe I was gonna hurt you because he hurt me. I don't want that to be the reason, because that's not right.

ARNOLD. No, you were going to hurt me because you have your honor to defend. Someone told you that I turned you in, you have no choice but to seek your revenge. If word got out that you didn't retaliate -- why everybody in school would start to challenge you. And then what kind of social order would we have?

BILL. For bein' such a genius, you sure are actin' real stupid.

ARNOLD. You're right, I'm actually trying to talk you into beating me up. *(They both laugh at that; BILL starts to leave.)*

ARNOLD. Where you going?

BILL. I'm gonna take you on your word that you're not a tattle -- that you didn't turn me in.

ARNOLD. I didn't, I swear. *(Beat.)* But what about the others?

BILL. You let me worry about that.

ARNOLD. And you have my word that I'm not going to say anything about what goes on over at your place.

BILL. Thanks. *(BILL starts to head out again.)*

ARNOLD. Bill, if you ever want to talk — You know, at night.

BILL. If I do, I'll look for ya' up on your roof. *(BILL exits. ARNOLD breathes a sigh of relief.)*

SCENE 12

(EMMA enters alone.)

EMMA. I screamed when the DJ told me I had not only won tickets to the concert, but backstage passes as well. *(She displays a backstage pass.)* I mean I had never won anything in my life, and then all of a sudden I was caller number twenty five and on my way to the biggest concert of the year! The New Landlords were my favorite group, and the fact that I was going to get to meet them kept me from getting much sleep the rest of the week. The concert was everything I hoped it would be, I had the best seat in the house and my friend Cindy owed me big time for giving her the other ticket. She just about passed out when we went backstage to meet the band members. Eddie was my favorite and I almost fainted when they introduced him to me. He was the lead singer, and not really that much older than me, even though he looked like he was. Cindy was so caught up with all the excitement, she didn't see Eddie and me leave the party and go to his dressing room. *(Pause.)* I guess I should have known what was going on, but I honestly thought we were just going to get away from the noise and have a good talk. Eddie and me alone together, it was like a dream or something! His lyrics are so inspiring, so full of love that I was completely shocked when he pulled me over to a couch and started tearing at my clothes. Maybe if he would have kissed me or something first I wouldn't have reacted like I did, but he moved on me so quick. He got on top of me and started pulling at my shirt. He was much stronger than me and even though I pushed and told him no, he pinned me down. I started to panic because I felt trapped and he wouldn't listen to me. His rough beard was scratching my face. His breath made me nauseous. When he started to unzip my pants it gave me just enough room to swing my knee hard into his crotch, causing him to fall off me. I got out of there before he could go any further. *(Pause.)* I saw him on MTV the next week. He had make-up on, but I could still see the scratch marks where I gouged his face. I hope they never heal. *(She looks at the backstage pass and tosses it on the ground as she exits.)*

SCENE 13

(CARMEN and JOANNE enter and cross down center.)

CARMEN. You want to open her locker?

JOANNE. Not really. You do it. *(CARMEN opens a combination lock, then opens the locker. They stare inside for a moment.)*

CARMEN. This is so weird.

JOANNE. Really.

CARMEN. I feel like I'm breaking in, or something.

JOANNE. She was always pretty protective of her locker.

CARMEN. Better us than her parents. Or especially better

than Vice Principal Adams. *(JOANNE starts to remove items; places them in a box.)*

JOANNE. She didn't have anything bad in here, did she?

CARMEN. I don't think so, not after they raided her locker last semester.

JOANNE. Yeah, she got in major trouble even though all they found was an empty bottle.

CARMEN. I'm surprised they only found one.

JOANNE. You shouldn't say stuff like that, especially now.

CARMEN. Maybe if I'd have said stuff like that to her, she might still be alive.

JOANNE. My Mom said I was lucky that I wasn't riding in the car with her. Or I'd probably be dead too.

CARMEN. That sounds like a Mom thing to say. Mine wasn't much better. She asked me if I ever got drunk with Cindy.

JOANNE. What did you tell her?

CARMEN. I didn't answer. And she didn't push it. *(JOANNE pulls out a small stuffed animal.)*

CARMEN. You gave her that for her birthday, didn't you?

JOANNE. Yeah.

CARMEN. You were the only one that gave her a present.

JOANNE. I can't believe her parents would forget something like that.

CARMEN. She told everyone that they were out of town.

JOANNE. Cindy was always covering for them.

CARMEN. You should keep it. It means something to you. She'd probably want you to have it. *(JOANNE pulls out a small journal.)*

CARMEN. *(Breaking a bit.)* Cin's journal. She wrote in that everyday. Remember what she called it?

JOANNE. "Shrink-in-a-box". She always felt better after

writing in it. *(Pause.)*

JOANNE. She ever let you read it?

CARMEN. Once. She just broke up with Jack and was pretty depressed. I asked her what was wrong and she just handed it to me to read.

JOANNE. Yeah. *(JOANNE thumbs through it.)*

JOANNE. There's something in here from Wednesday. The same day --

CARMEN. Let's not read it. Those were her private thoughts. It's not right that anybody reads it -- especially her Mom.

JOANNE. But I told her we'd bring everything over to the house.

CARMEN. She'll never know.

JOANNE. I got an idea -- let's slip it in her casket. You know, tonight at the Funeral Home, when no one is looking.

CARMEN. *(Forcing a smile.)* That's a real Cindy thing to do. She'd like that. *(Pause.)* We better go through all her papers and stuff. In case there's something else she wouldn't want her Mom to see.

JOANNE. Right. We can go over to my place first and sort through everything. *(JOANNE removes a stack of books.)*

JOANNE. *(Sad laugh.)* Look at these books, they're like new.

CARMEN. Cin never was much to study or anything.

JOANNE. This locker was so important to her.

CARMEN. It was her home base.

JOANNE. This makes everything so final. I really miss her.

CARMEN. Me, too.

JOANNE. The rest of this year is going to be pretty lame without her around.

CARMEN. Yeah.

JOANNE. It just won't be the same. *(A BELL is heard.)*

CARMEN. Let's get outta here before all the "looky loos" start hangin' around.

JOANNE. I've had enough of them. *(CARMEN scoops the rest of the items into the box.)*

JOANNE. Put the lock back on. I think it should stay empty the rest of the year.

CARMEN. I agree. *(JOANNE picks up the box and starts to head off; CARMEN puts the lock back on and pauses for a moment.)*

JOANNE. Are you coming?

CARMEN. Yeah. *(CARMEN places her open palm on the closed locker as a parting gesture and then exits with JOANNE.)*

SCENE 14

DANNY. *(Enters.)* Who would have ever thought that she would be mine? That I, Danny Logan, would ever have such a beauty all to myself. After looking at her for years, after wanting her for years, she is finally mine. And beautiful? When I'm with her, others turn their heads as we go by. It's her body. A perfect 10. She's older than me, but you'd never know it – and she's very powerful. What an incredible combination, beauty and power. It's a sign that I am no longer Danny Logan, the little kid next door, but Dan Logan, a man who has something that all other men only wish for. She is mine for now and forever. She has changed my life – A 1976 Chevy Camaro and she's all mine!

SCENE 15

(WANDA sits wiping tears from her eyes, TABITHA enters and crosses to her.)

TABITHA. I don't have to ask. It's pretty obvious you told Scott.

WANDA. Yes I did.

TABITHA. How did he take it?

WANDA. A lot harder than I thought he would, that's why I'm so upset. I think I really hurt him.

TABITHA. Hey, don't feel guilty. He hurt you plenty of times.

WANDA. You're right. Just like you were right about me breaking up with him -- I should have done it months ago.

TABITHA. He was using you.

WANDA. I know that. Well, not at first, but after you explained it to me -- it really made things clear.

TABITHA. I didn't want to, but I figured since I was a friend and all -- I owed that to you.

WANDA. You're the best friend ever.

TABITHA. It just made me so mad how he would lie to you, cheat on you, and take you for granted.

WANDA. How could I have been so stupid not to see it myself?

TABITHA. Love does that to you, it gets in the way of things.

WANDA. It's like you said, I didn't really love Scott, I was just in love with the idea of being in love.

TABITHA. Exactly, even though you knew you were in a bad relationship, it was better than no relationship at all.

WANDA. I was.

TABITHA. You don't need him anymore.

WANDA. No I don't. And that's exactly what I told him. "Scott, I don't need you anymore."

TABITHA. And he took it hard, huh?

WANDA. Real hard. For a minute I almost changed my mind and took him back, but I kept remembering what you told me. That gave me strength.

TABITHA. If you would've folded, you would've been stuck with him for maybe the rest of your life.

WANDA. Scott is a jerk, and thank God you were there to point that out to me.

TABITHA. He's all looks and nothing else.

WANDA. A pretty package with no contents.

TABITHA. Nice building, no inventory.

WANDA. Good acting, bad script.

TABITHA. A limousine with a four cylinder engine. *(WANDA gives her a double take on that.)*

TABITHA. So it's over for you two?

WANDA. Completely. It was a big scene. He screamed, I screamed. He cried, I cried. Everybody saw it.

TABITHA. That's good, then it makes it final.

WANDA. Very final. *(SCOTT approaches.)*

TABITHA. Maybe not, here he comes now.

WANDA. Oh, no.

TABITHA. Be strong, don't give in.

SCOTT. Hi Tabitha.

TABITHA. Hi Scott.

SCOTT. Wanda —

WANDA. Scott, I don't even want to argue about it. *(WANDA looks to TABITHA who gives her a nod of encouragement.)*

SCOTT. I'm not here to argue, I wanted to give you your

CD's back -- they were in my locker. *(He hands her several Compact Discs.)*

WANDA. Oh -- well, thank you.

SCOTT. So, I guess we won't be going to the Cobra's concert this weekend.

WANDA. I think you know the answer to that.

SCOTT. Even though I already bought the tickets for us.

WANDA. *(Looks to Tabitha.)* Uh -- NO. It wouldn't be right.

SCOTT. How about you, Tabitha? You want to go?

TABITHA. Sure. *(TABITHA stands and crosses to him.)* What time you gonna pick me up?

SCOTT. Early, so we can get some dinner first. *(They start walking away.)*

TABITHA. How about that new Chinese place that opened in the mall?

SCOTT. Sounds good to me. *(They are now gone, leaving a very confused WANDA sitting alone.)*

SCENE 16

(ANNIE YEAGER sits nervously waiting to see the Principal, she is surprised when DENISE LOWELL enters and sit next to her.)

ANNIE. Denise? What are you doing here?

DENISE. Mr. Kelsey kicked me out of class.

ANNIE. You were kicked out of class? Miss National Honor Society. Miss Class President. Miss everything, except Miss Behave.

DENISE. Well, today I crossed over to the other side -- way

over.

ANNIE. What happened?

DENISE. "Into the World Came A Soul Named Ida."

ANNIE. Ida who?

DENISE. It's a famous painting of a homely woman -- some say she's a prostitute.

ANNIE. Wow, I'm taking the wrong classes here.

DENISE. It was question #5 on our mid-term final. "Explain the meaning of the painting 'Into The World Came A Soul Named Ida'."

ANNIE. And he got mad because you called Ida a hooker?

DENISE. He got mad because I didn't. I didn't see her that way and I told him he had no right marking my answer wrong, just because I disagreed with him.

ANNIE. What did you disagree on?

DENISE. He saw Ida as a common whore, who painted herself up and struck out into the night in search of quick money.

ANNIE. How did you see her?

DENISE. I saw her as a symbol of what being a woman has always been about. The fact that we are forced to become something other than what we want to be. Ida was ugly, and looked down on by society. She was a victim of her own insecurity, but that didn't make her a whore. She was struggling in a world that imposed its values on her, just as Mr. Kelsey was imposing his views on us. And he told me I was wrong! It was my interpretation. How can I be wrong? He can expose us to paintings, but how dare he insist that we agree with what he says they mean. Suddenly something inside of me just kinda snapped. And then I told Mr. Kelsey that he could never understand what Ida represented because he was a chauvinistic pig who was still living in the 19th century with his macho head up his butt. *(Calmer.)* That's when he kicked me out.

ANNIE. You really said that to him?

DENISE. Yes, I did.

ANNIE. Whoa, and you're not even a Senior yet. *(Pause.)*

DENISE. What did you get in trouble for?

ANNIE. I'm embarrassed to say after what you told me.

DENISE. Don't be embarrassed, we all have our causes.

ANNIE. I skipped out of 3rd period History class and went to 7-11 for a Slurpee. *(Pause.)*

VOICE OF PRINCIPAL. *(Offstage.)* Miss Yeager – ANNIE! *(ANNIE gets up and starts to exit. She stops and turns back to DENISE.)*

ANNIE. But – uh – *(Proud.)* I did it to protest how we women have been treated throughout history. *(She gives a thumbs up to DENISE, and then exits.)*

SCENE 17

(GERALD works on his lap-top computer; LINDA enters.)

LINDA. Don't even tell me you didn't do it, because I know that you did.

GERALD. *(Amused.)* Did what?

LINDA. You hacked the school's computer.

GERALD.   There's nothing hack about me, I'm a professional.

LINDA. Yes, a professional criminal.

GERALD. No one will ever find out.

LINDA. *I* found out.

GERALD. Only because I wanted you to. *(She takes out a piece of paper; looks at it.)*

LINDA. I can't believe this.

GERALD. How does it feel to get straight "A's" ?

LINDA. Like I'm looking at someone else's report card, that's how it feels.

GERALD. I was going to give you a couple of "B's", but then I thought -- what the heck. Let's live a little.

LINDA. They're going to find out about this.

GERALD. Never.

LINDA. Yes they will, because I'm going right down to the office and tell them.

GERALD. I don't think you will.

LINDA. What makes you so sure?

GERALD. Scenario. Your house last night. "Linda, come in here, your Mother and I want to talk to you about your report card." Nervously you walk into the family den, head held low, sweat beads starting to form on your forehead. Knowing that the highest mark you earned was a "C", and that was in Band. Lifting your head, you become confused to see your parents smiling -- beaming with pride. "We are so proud of you -- we knew you could do it." The hugs, the praise, and let me guess. Money? A trip? Maybe even a shopping spree at the mall? All of this, because of a few strokes on the keyboard from yours truly. No way will you give all of that up.

LINDA. You're out of your mind.

GERALD. Very much in, thank you.

LINDA. But why? That's what I can't understand. Why did you do it?

GERALD. Because I wanted to ask you out next weekend.

LINDA. You wanted to ask me out?

GERALD. On a date, you may have low grades -- but I'm sure you know what a date is.

LINDA. You broke into the computer room because you wanted to ask me out?

GERALD. I didn't break in -- I have a key.

LINDA. And you thought by fixing my report card, I'd then want to go out with you?

GERALD. You now owe me.

LINDA. Owe you?

GERALD. It's a matter of logic. Like a computer game. It merely lowers the risk of failure.

LINDA. I don't believe this. It just doesn't work that way.

GERALD. It always has before.

LINDA. You've done this before?

GERALD. Four times. And those girls were all appreciative. They were glad I did it.

LINDA. Well I'm different.

GERALD. Come on, you can't tell me that you didn't love seeing all those high grades. And now that you know how talented I am, don't I look a lot better to you?

LINDA. Gerald, let me explain something to you. I don't date guys because of what they do for me. I date guys because I want to be with them.

GERALD. So, now you want to be with me, right?

LINDA. No! As a matter of fact, I want to turn you in for the slime-ball that you are.

GERALD. I'll deny everything.

LINDA. I'm sure you would.

GERALD. If you tell the office, then your parents will know your real grades.

LINDA. They already do. I told them that there was a mistake on my report card. Like maybe the computer burped or something.

GERALD. Computers don't burp.

LINDA. Well, they bought it. And they were pretty disappointed with the truth. I think it made my real grades sound even worse.

GERALD. That's your own fault.

LINDA. My fault?

GERALD. You could have good grades for the rest of the year if you want. And that's not all. How about airline tickets? A credit line at the store of your choice? Free phone calls? You name it and me and my little computer can create it.

LINDA. You are one sick puppy.

GERALD. You know, you're different from the rest. I didn't enter your attitude into the equation. I really thought I had you figured out.

LINDA. Gerald, you don't even have yourself figured out. *(She exits.)*

GERALD. So does this mean you aren't going to go out with me?

SCENE 18

(SUE POWELL enters.)

SUE POWELL. *(Smug.)* I was picked as the Homecoming Queen, and you weren't. *(She exits.)*

SCENE 19

MIKE. My name is Mike. Some of you know me as Cougar, 'cause that was the name given to me by the gang. Well, it wasn't given to me, I had to earn it by doin' crimes. Like robbin' some guy over on 7th street. He was walkin' on our sidewalk. It was like he was askin' for it. I showed him my loaded 9 -- and he gave up his cash. 'Cause nobody's gonna disrespect me on my own turf when I got my gun. Nobody. *(Pause.)* And then the school here put in those damn metal detectors and I had to leave my gun at home during the day. At home where my little brother found it and decided to play with it. He must have seen me put it under the mattress when I wasn't lookin'. Jesus, he was too young to know what that thing could do -- to him it was just a toy. *(Pause.)* I was the one that found his body. The ambulance took a long time to get to him. Ambulances always take a long time in my part of town. But it didn't matter anyway. Oh God, how did he get in my room? I locked the door. I mean I really thought I locked the door. What the hell was he doin' in there anyway? *(Long pause.)* Look, don't call me Cougar. I don't want that name no more. 'Cause my little brother didn't call me that. He didn't know who Cougar was. My little brother -- he knew me only as Mike.

SCENE 20

CHRISTIAN. When I was a kid, my teachers told my parents that I had a bad temper. It was so much easier to deal with then. But now things have changed. Now I have a Psychiatrist who says that I suffer from "Spontaneous

Emotional Episodes", which basically means – I have a bad temper. And what did this genius, who gets paid $100 an hour, suggest I do to overcome my disorder? SOCKS. He said that I should put a sock on my hand, and have it represent the person I'm upset with. I'm supposed to tell that sock everything that bothers me about our relationship and not hold anything back. So I took his advice and focused on one person that made me angrier than all the rest. *(He puts a bright red sock on his left hand.)* I call him Dr. Shaffer, my Psychiatrist. *(To sock.)* Listen you overeducated, lay down on my couch, blame everything on my Mother, $100 an hour, out of shape, frustrated Freud, long word using, can't get your own act together dork! I'm sick of going to your office just because I happen to get a little mad at people once and awhile and having you make me feel like I'm some sort of serial killer. *(Makes sock talk.)* "But Christian, you have to learn to control your anger before you enter the real world." *(To sock.)* By wearing a stupid sock on my hand and talking to it like it was a person? Is that what they do in the real world? Are you trying to heal me, or train me to be a ventriloquist? You jerk! *(Pause; takes sock off his hand.)* You know something – maybe he's right. I do feel a lot better.

SCENE 21

(NOEL and GRANT play catch with a football. ALLISON, a rather timid girl with glasses, enters and watches for a moment.)

ALLISON. Grant, can I talk to you?
GRANT. You already are.

ALLISON. I mean alone.

NOEL. Whoa — *(He laughs suggestively, causing ALLISON to shoot him a dirty look.)*

GRANT. *(To NOEL.)* I'll catch up with you later, Noel.

NOEL. All right, but if I run into Jacqueline, I may just have to tell her about you two.

GRANT. Get lost. *(NOEL leaves, but not before giving ALLISON another heckling laugh.)*

GRANT. You got two minutes.

ALLISON. I should have said something in front of him — I should have said something in front of the whole class.

GRANT. What are you talkin' about?

ALLISON. I saw you Grant Arthur — I saw you cheating on the test this morning.

GRANT. That's bull, I didn't cheat on no test.

ALLISON. I sit right behind you, I saw you copy from Kenneth. You weren't even subtle about it. He would write his answer, and then you'd copy, he'd write, you'd copy — you even turned your test in right after he did.

GRANT. I don't have to take this from you. *(He starts to leave.)*

ALLISON. If I don't get some answers, I'll go to Mr. Martin and tell him. All he has to do is compare your tests and he'd know. *(GRANT stops.)*

GRANT. So you saw me copying off someone's test. What do you care? I didn't copy off from you.

ALLISON. Oh, then it shouldn't matter because I wasn't involved?

GRANT. Yeah, what's it to you?

ALLISON. Because I studied last night, that's why.

GRANT. What?

ALLISON. I know you won't believe this, but I have a life,

too. There was a movie I wanted to go to last night, but I couldn't because I had to stay home and study "mitosis".

GRANT. Mitosis?

ALLISON. Mitosis -- It was the 7th question on the test, you wrote down "C", which was the correct answer.

GRANT. How do you know I wrote down "C"? Were you copying off my paper?

ALLISON. Don't twist this around -- I studied.

GRANT. I remember about Mitosis. Mr. Martin showed that movie. The nucleus of a cell divides in half and each of the halves contain the same number of chromosomes.

ALLISON. *(Surprised.)* That's right.

GRANT. I know.

ALLISON. If you knew that, than why did you have to copy Kenneth's test?

GRANT. Maybe I just did it for grins.

ALLISON. Grins?

GRANT. Yeah, as a joke.

ALLISON. I don't buy that for a minute. Why did you cheat?

GRANT. *(Impatient.)* The same reason I cheat on every test I take.

ALLISON. Don't tell me, you're worried about getting kicked off the football team. You jocks are all alike.

GRANT. You're way out of line.

ALLISON. *(Angry.)* If that isn't the reason, then what is?

GRANT. *(Returning anger.)* If you really have to know, it's because I can't read.

ALLISON. What? *(GRANT looks around to make sure no one heard him.)*

GRANT. Look, if you want to turn me in, go ahead. Just leave me alone. *(He starts to exit.)*

ALLISON. Wait. *(He stops; ALLISON crosses to him.)*

ALLISON. I'm not going to turn you in. It just made me a little angry when I saw you get away with it, that's all.

GRANT. Yeah, well I've been getting away with it for a long time.

ALLISON. You really can't read?

GRANT. I can read – a little. Easy stuff. But it takes me awhile and tests use a lot big words. Listen, I shouldn't have said anything. You tricked me.

ALLISON. If you're worried about me telling anyone, forget it. I'm not like that. I just can't imagine that someone who's gone to school as long as you wouldn't be able to read.

GRANT. It's easier than you think.

ALLISON. They have special programs that could help.

GRANT. And what do they call kids that go to those special programs?

ALLISON. *(Sarcastic.)* Wouldn't want people to make fun of you, I mean being so popular and all.

GRANT. So, are you pissed because I cheated on the test, or because I'm popular?

ALLISON. I'm sorry, I didn't mean it that way.

GRANT. Look, if it makes you feel better. Next test Martin gives, I'll flunk it.

ALLISON. That won't make me feel better.

GRANT. Then what do you want from me? *(Pause.)*

ALLISON. Let me help you.

GRANT. Help me?

ALLISON. I could help you to read – better, I mean.

GRANT. No way.

ALLISON. No one would need to know, you could come over to my place. We've got a guest house out back that no one ever uses. We could work there.

GRANT. It's too late, maybe a few years ago.

ALLISON. Grant, you're a very smart guy, I can tell. It wouldn't take long — I know it wouldn't.

GRANT. But what if someone finds out?

ALLISON. You've gone all this time and no one did.

GRANT. I'll have to think about this.

ALLISON. All right, I won't push it. But you'd also be doing me a favor.

GRANT. How?

ALLISON. I plan on teaching someday, it would be good practice.

GRANT. Yeah, well — like I said, I'll think about it.

ALLISON. Okay. *(She starts to head off.)*

GRANT. Allison?

ALLISON. Yes?

GRANT. We got a game tonight, but — how about tomorrow around eight?

ALLISON. That would be fine.

GRANT. Great — and, uh, thanks. *(GRANT looks around, then exits.)*

SCENE 22

(PAMELA and JENNIFER enter.)

JENNIFER. Do you mind if I sit down?

PAMELA. Maybe you need some food.

JENNIFER. The cafeteria is too crowded.

PAMELA. So we make room, I think you should eat.

JENNIFER. Just give me a minute here. I mean I've only been out of the hospital a few days.

PAMELA. Yeah, but you're fine now.

JENNIFER. Do you think I look pale?

PAMELA. Not anymore than usual. I swear you're part albino.

JENNIFER. I don't know. Kim told me I looked pale.

PAMELA. She spends her life out in the sun, everybody looks pale to her. Let's go eat. *(PAMELA starts to leave, JENNIFER doesn't move.)*

JENNIFER. You didn't say anything to anybody, did you?

PAMELA. I told you I wouldn't.

JENNIFER. People have been treating me different.

PAMELA. You've had two weeks off from school, they're just jealous.

JENNIFER. I feel so different. Just like that I'm some kind of freak.

PAMELA. Come on, you have Diabetes. Lot's of people have it. My Aunt has it.

JENNIFER. You're Aunt doesn't go to this High School.

PAMELA. I think the best thing for you is to eat lunch with me and catch up on all the gossip.

JENNIFER. I don't really want to be around a lot of people right now.

PAMELA. What about all your friends? *(Pointed.)* What about Todd? You can't avoid him for very long. This school isn't that big.

JENNIFER. I'm not avoiding Todd.

PAMELA. He thinks you are.

JENNIFER. You talked to him?

PAMELA. Third period.

JENNIFER. You didn't say anything about -- if you said anything --

PAMELA. Easy, easy. I promised you I wouldn't and my

word is good. I don't have much else, that at least is still worth something.

JENNIFER. What did he say?

PAMELA. He thinks you don't like him anymore.

JENNIFER. Oh, God. He's so insecure sometimes.

PAMELA. Insecure? You miss two weeks of school, don't return his calls, and then when you come back to school you're like the Invisible Woman or something.

JENNIFER. I'm just not ready to tell him yet.

PAMELA. What's to tell? So you have to take a few shots. *(Dramatic.)* With great big needles! *(JENNIFER shoots her a look.)*

PAMELA. Just kidding. Geez, I'm just trying to lighten things up here.

JENNIFER. You make it sound like I caught a cold or something. I'm a little scared, okay. Two weeks ago everything was fine, then I get the flu and all of a sudden I'm being rushed to the hospital and they tell me I have some kind of disease that I know nothing about. I thought it was because I ate too much candy, but they say it has something to do with genetics and blood lines and stuff I don't want to think of. The next thing I know I'm sticking a syringe into an orange and watching tapes of blind people with their legs cut off. Excuse me if I think it is a big deal.

PAMELA. Todd really cares about you, Jennifer. He's hurting right now.

JENNIFER. And you think if I tell him I have a major disease, that will make everything all right?

PAMELA. Something like that.

JENNIFER. And the two of us will just go on being boyfriend and girlfriend like nothing has happened.

PAMELA. Why not?

JENNIFER.   Your Aunt's diabetic -- so is my cousin. Thought everything was going to be fine, until one night during a Valentine's Dance she passed out on the dance floor and they had to call the paramedics.   Her boyfriend was real understanding -- he understood it was too embarrassing to be with her in public. Dropped her within a week.

PAMELA. So your cousin went with a jerk, you're going with Todd.

JENNIFER. Why did this have to happen to me?

PAMELA. Look at the bright side, at least you got a great excuse to get out of gym class when Miss Ulmer gets her panties in a wad. *(JENNIFER stifles a laugh on that.)*

PAMELA. He's going to find out -- it might as well be from you.

JENNIFER. Do you know where he is --

PAMELA. Cafeteria, third table, second seat -- but I didn't tell him why you were going to meet him.

JENNIFER. You set me up.

PAMELA. Guilty.

JENNIFER. Oh, you are so sneaky.

PAMELA. Come on, I'll even give up my dessert in honor of you.

JENNIFER.   Wow, now that really touches my heart. *(JENNIFER puts her arm around PAMELA; leads her off.)*

PAMELA. But just for lunch. Tonight I plan on pigging out on cookies, a hot fudge sundae, frozen yogurt topped with Gummi Bears, crushed oreos -- *(They are now gone.)*

SCENE 23

(ALLEN paces, MARISA sits.)

ALLEN. What's taking them so long? We should have known an hour ago.

MARISA. Maybe it's closer than you think.

ALLEN. Maybe it's such a landslide that they have to think of a nice way to break the news to you.

MARISA. You're pretty confident.

ALLEN. I'm the best man for the job.

MARISA. Best *man*?

ALLEN. You know what I mean – but leave it to you to try to twist everything I say, just like you did throughout the whole campaign.

MARISA. I may have twisted, but I never lied like you did.

ALLEN. Name one thing I lied about.

MARISA. Matching funds for field trips – longer lunch periods – your scholastic record –

ALLEN. I said name one thing.

MARISA. So you admit to those lies?

ALLEN. They weren't lies, they were campaign promises -- if the President of the United States can stretch the truth, why not the President of the Senior Class?

MARISA. They haven't elected you yet.

ALLEN. They will. *(Pause.)*

ALLEN. Listen, I know the campaign got a little rough –

MARISA. A little rough? You spray painted graffiti on my car, you appointed my ex-boyfriend as your campaign advisor so you could dig up dirt on me, and you spread rumors that I was having an affair with the School Superintendent.

ALLEN. You do spend a lot of time in his office.

MARISA. My Mother is his Secretary.

ALLEN. Hey, that's politics.

MARISA. You're nothing but a SLIME-BALL. You ran a very dirty campaign.

ALLEN. You're starting to sound like a sore loser. Does that mean you're conceding?

MARISA. Never.

ALLEN. You have to admit, I'm exactly what the Senior Class needs.

MARISA. A loud mouth, self-important, jerk?

ALLEN. Name me one politician who isn't.

MARISA. What our class needs is someone who can make some positive changes.

ALLEN. Campaign's over. Save it for your next failed attempt at Government.

MARISA. Failed attempt? What about you? As I remember, you ran for President, and lost, for the past three years.

ALLEN. Not true. My Sophomore year I ran for Treasurer.

MARISA. That's right, Treasurer. Now I remember -- and I voted for you.

ALLEN. You did?

MARISA. I thought you were the best *person* for the job.

ALLEN. Really?

MARISA. Really.

ALLEN. Why did you think that?

MARISA. We were both in Geometry class. It was a Tuesday -- I remember the day because Mr. Talma was giving his weekly pop quiz. You sat a few seats in front of me and right behind Linda Jansen. She had slung her purse across the back of her chair and a twenty dollar bill fell out. You picked it up and stuffed it back in her purse. Didn't even tell her about it, just put it back in her purse.

ALLEN. See, I'm a wonderful guy.

MARISA. You were back then, but you've changed.

ALLEN. Just because I play the politician doesn't mean I'm like that for real.

MARISA. I don't think you can separate the two?

ALLEN. What about you? You pretend to be so honest, and so pure. What's in this for you?

MARISA. What do you mean?

ALLEN. Nobody runs for office, even in High School, without wanting something in return. Is it power? Is it greed? Or is it knowing that everyone will kiss your butt for favors?

MARISA. You have an evil mind.

ALLEN. Maybe, but at least I'm willing to admit my lust for power.

MARISA. I want to be Class President to help my fellow students.

ALLEN. I don't believe you. And that's what bothers you the most about me. *(A STUDENT enters.)*

STUDENT. Congratulations Marisa, you're the new Class President. *(Long pause; MARISA is as stunned as ALLEN.)*

ALLEN. How close was it?

STUDENT. Well, we're not really supposed to tell.

ALLEN. *(Angry.)* I demand a recount. *(To STUDENT.)* Especially if you had anything to do with counting the votes.

STUDENT. Oh yeah, well if you really have to know, she creamed you. You only got about 10% of the votes. *(STUDENT leaves.)*

MARISA. Allen, I'm sorry.

ALLEN. No you're not. *(Pause.)* Aw, what the hell -- the people have spoken. *(He starts to leave.)*

MARISA. Wait. You were right. I did want this position for a reason. I thought it would look good on my record -- that a college might give me special consideration because of it.

ALLEN. Well, maybe there's hope for you yet.

MARISA. You know I really didn't think I'd win.

ALLEN. Neither did I.

MARISA. It's a big responsibility. I'm a little naive about all of this. I could use your help.

ALLEN. My help? You called me a slime-ball.

MARISA. You are -- I mean part of you is. And that's why I need your help.

ALLEN. What's in it for me?

MARISA. As much power as I can throw your way.

ALLEN. You've only been in office for a few minutes, and you've already made your first good decision.

SCENE 24

(ADAM spots VERA, runs to her and gives her a big kiss.)

VERA. I've missed you.

ADAM. How long has it been?

VERA. Almost ten hours.

ADAM. That's too long.

VERA. Way too long. *(ADAM notices her small diamond ring.)*

ADAM. I thought you weren't going to wear that.

VERA. Not at home, but I'm going to here at school.

ADAM. Aren't you afraid that someone will find out?

VERA. To tell you the truth, I'm afraid someone won't.

ADAM. I still think we should just tell our parents.

VERA. You know I do too, but we both agreed that your Dad would freak.

ADAM. No, my Mom would freak, my Dad would probably disown me.

VERA. They're gonna really hate me when they find out.

ADAM. Then it's their problem, not yours.

VERA. Especially now that I'm their daughter-in-law. *(ADAM takes a couple of steps away.)*

VERA. What's wrong?

ADAM. It's not fair to ask you to be my wife and then pretend that we're still just dating.

VERA. We've been all through this. It's only for a couple more months, then we're both 18 and nobody can say nothing.

ADAM. You're right.

VERA. No, *we're* right.

ADAM. So do you feel any different?

VERA. I didn't think I would, but when I woke up today -- I can't even describe it.

ADAM. You don't have to -- been there, done that.

VERA. You don't regret it, do you?

ADAM. No way, it's perfect. We're perfect.

VERA. I still want a big wedding, you know.

ADAM. I know. You want the beauty of an old fashioned wedding.

VERA. No, I want the appliances and money and stuff.

ADAM. *(Smiling.)* Now I see.

VERA. Besides, keeping this thing a secret, you know, living each day like a mystery -- it's so romantic.

ADAM. I never looked at it like that before. It is kinda like a movie or somethin'.

VERA. One with a very happy ending. *(They look at each*

other for a moment. Then they embrace and kiss.)

VERA. It will always be like this, won't it Adam.

ADAM. Always. *(He puts his arm around her and they exit.)*

SCENE 25

(DEIDRA and BRENT sit next to each other; each wears a Graduation Cap and robe.)

VOICE. *(Offstage.)* As you travel down the road of life, you will find that the years spent here at this school will become a foundation for your success. In the future, when you look back, you will remember these to be the best of times and the worst of times -- *(VOICE fades.)*

DEIDRA. *(Whispers.)* I can't believe we made it. Finally after 12 years of sitting in classes, we are free. First thing I'm gonna do is sleep until noon tomorrow. *(Pause.)* God this speaker is boring, why did they get him?

BRENT. He's a Politician.

DEIDRA. Personally I think they should have gotten a VJ from MTV -- that's someone I'd listen to.

BRENT. It's not for us, it's for our parents.

DEIDRA. My Mom watches MTV.

BRENT. Your Mom's not a typical parent.

DEIDRA. Besides, I thought he was supposed to speak before we got our diplomas.

BRENT. He was late getting here -- they flew him in on a helicopter.

DEIDRA. When you're a kid and your late it's called being tardy -- when you get older it's called being important.

BRENT. Yeah, right.

DEIDRA. You having a party tonight?

BRENT. No.

DEIDRA. Saving it for the weekend so all the relatives will come?

BRENT. Well, uh, not exactly.

DEIDRA. I'm having mine tonight, you can come over if you want. I can't wait to score all that cash.

BRENT. At least you're honest.

DEIDRA. So are your parents going to get you that car like they promised?

BRENT. Not for awhile.

DEIDRA. You oughta sue 'em. They promised you a car when you graduated. They can't back out of a deal like that.

BRENT. They haven't backed out. I didn't graduate yet.

DEIDRA. What are you talking about? We just picked up our diplomas. Of course you graduated.

BRENT. Mine's not signed.

DEIDRA. What do you mean it's not signed? *(He shows her.)*

DEIDRA. It's not signed.

BRENT. Just like I said. *(DEIDRA looks at her own diploma.)*

DEIDRA. Mine is -- they must have made some mistake on yours.

BRENT. It was no mistake. I'm a credit short. I have to go to summer school.

DEIDRA. How can you be a credit short?

BRENT. I flunked Spanish class.

DEIDRA. I thought you said you were passing all of your classes.

BRENT. I thought I was too.

DEIDRA. When did you find out?

BRENT. Two days ago. My parents got a letter in the mail.

DEIDRA. A letter?

BRENT. I wasn't too happy about that either. Here I am, eighteen years old – old enough to vote, but I guess not old enough to handle this kind of news.

DEIDRA. They're probably afraid you wouldn't tell your parents about it.

BRENT. One thing's for sure, I sure wouldn't have until after I got the car.

DEIDRA. That bites, just because you flunked Spanish. I could see if it was English, but Spanish? What's that matter?

BRENT. I guess now since most of our jobs are going to Mexico, it's really important.

DEIDRA. You got a point there.

BRENT. I really didn't want to be here today, but the school sorta made me.

DEIDRA. They made you come to the ceremony, even though you're not done yet? That's cruel.

BRENT. They told my parents I should be here since they don't have a graduation ceremony in August. Besides, my Mom already bought a new dress for today – that's what she was the most pissed about.

DEIDRA. Well, she got to wear it then. What about your dad?

BRENT. He's pretty disappointed in me. He didn't say much, but I can tell because he didn't bring his video camera. He takes that everywhere. I heard him tell my Mom he didn't want any footage of me receiving an unsigned diploma.

DEIDRA. No one would have to know, it's not like that would show on the video.

BRENT. I'm glad he's not recording this. I don't need to be reminded ten years from now what a loser I was.

DEIDRA. You're not a loser.

BRENT. Easy for you to say, your diploma is signed.

(They both stand up. They are joined by all of the other CAST MEMBERS, who also wear graduation caps and gowns. They all form a line across the stage, facing the audience; DEIDRA and BRENT are in the center.)

DEIDRA. Hey, look – I'm pretty good at Spanish. If you want, I could tutor you this summer.

BRENT. I may need that.

DEIDRA. As long as it's not before noon.

BRENT. Don't rub it in.

VOICE. *(Offstage.)* The world is your oyster and it's up to each and every one of you to open it up and grab hold of the pearl that you've worked so hard for. My respect and encouragement goes out to you the class of _____!

(All the CAST MEMBERS remove their graduation caps and throw them into the air, as the LIGHTS fade to BLACK.)

END

Also by
Brad Slaight...

Copies

High Tide and Sightings

Middle Class

The Road Taken

Second Class

OTHER TITLES AVAILABLE FROM BAKER's PLAYS

MIDDLE CLASS

Brad Slaight

10 Students - 4m, 6f / Flexible Cast / Simple Set

Middle Class is a continuation of the popular "class" play cycle written especially for young actors by Brad Slaight. Like the earlier *Class Action* and *Second Class*, *Middle Class* explores the tribulations of young people while in school. Where the other two plays dealt with high school aged characters, Middle Class concerns a group of young people in a modern middle school (junior high). Incorporating an ensemble of players, taking on numerous roles, the play offers insight (often humorous, often poignant) into the issues facing young people during the complex transition from grade school to high school. Such themes as identity, personal relations, status, expectations, and competitiveness are central to the play.

Middle Class was commissioned by the Young Conservatory at the Tony Award winning American Conservatory Theater (A.C.T.) in San Francisco.

CPSIA information can be obtained at www.ICGtesting.com
Printed in the USA
LVOW13s1015021013

355070LV00001B/3/P